IS THAT YOU
MRS PINKERTON-TRUNKS?
AND OTHER STORIES FROM
'GET UP AND GO'

IS THAT YOU
MRS PINKERTON-TRUNKS?

AND OTHER STORIES FROM
'GET UP AND GO'

Shirley Isherwood
Introduced by Beryl Reid

Illustrated by Maureen Roffey

HUTCHINSON
London Melbourne Sydney Auckland Johannesburg

Hutchinson Children's Books Ltd

An imprint of the Hutchinson Publishing Group

17–21 Conway Street, London W1P 6JD

Hutchinson Publishing Group (Australia) Pty Ltd
PO Box 496, 16–22 Church Street, Hawthorne, Melbourne, Victoria 3122

Hutchinson Group (NZ) Ltd
32–34 View Road, PO Box 40-086, Glenfield, Auckland 10

Hutchinson Group (SA) Pty Ltd
PO Box 337, Bergvlei 2012, South Africa

First published 1984

Set in Baskerville by BookEns, Saffron Walden, Essex
Made and printed in Great Britain by
Anchor Brendon Ltd, Tiptree, Essex

British Library Cataloguing in Publication Data

Isherwood, Shirley
Is that you, Mrs Pinkerton-Trunks?
I. Title
823'.914 [J]   PZ7

ISBN 0 09 156370 4

Contents

Introduction

I have always enjoyed telling stories, especially to children – it's not often you have a proper excuse to rediscover that magical childhood world where the real and imaginary merge. So when Yorkshire Television asked me to present the 'Get Up and Go!' storytime series, I was delighted.

The stories are enchanting, and getting to know the characters week by week was a real joy. They all have their own very distinctive personalities: Mr Milford-Haven, not the cleverest lion in the world (as you will discover in *Upside Down* and *Flying*), but a lion whose heart is definitely in the right place; Mrs Pinkerton-Trunks, a very practical and talented elephant, who seems able to turn her trunk to anything; Monkey, who is a bit mischievous and secretive; and Woodley, a real dog with a mind of his own, who often has the answers to the many problems that present themselves, if anyone would ever

7

listen to him! At the centre of things there is Billie, the little girl to whom the animals belong and who is always around to keep an eye on them.

Apart from the humour, which children love and which makes the stories such fun for adults to read aloud, I think the reason the stories are so successful is that they are all firmly rooted in the everyday happenings of a small child's world – from what to do on a rainy day and first bicycle rides, to lost tortoises and playing hide-and-seek.

I have had tremendous fun telling the stories for 'Get Up and Go!' and am so pleased that, with the publication of this book, parents and children can now share these magical tales at home. And, as Mrs Pinkerton-Trunks would say, 'What could be nicer, dear?'

Beryl Reid

Billie's Toys

Once upon a time there was a little girl called Billie, who lived with her father. One day, when Billie was three years old, her father bought her a lion. He was big and cuddly, and his name was Mr Milford-Haven.

Billie loved Mr Milford-Haven. She carried him with her wherever she went, and at night he lay at the foot of her bed. Sometimes, just before she went to sleep, Billie thought she heard him growl, and sometimes she thought she heard him purr, like a big yellow cat. 'Mr Milford-Haven,' she whispered, 'is that you?' But Mr Milford-Haven just lay there, with his great golden mane tumbled over his eyes, and his big velvet paws side by side on the bedcover.

The next year, when Billie was four, her father bought her a monkey. He was brown and fat, and he wore a little white T-shirt. Billie loved Monkey, and wherever she and Mr Milford-Haven went, Monkey went too.

At night Monkey sat on the table by Billie's bed. Sometimes, just before she went to sleep, Billie thought she heard him scampering round the room – but in the morning there he was, sitting on the table and staring at her with his bright, round eyes.

When Christmas came, Billie's father gave her a big, grey elephant, called Mrs Pinkerton-Trunks. She was a beautiful elephant! She wore a little red hat, with daisies round the brim, and a woollen shawl around her shoulders. She carried a handbag, and inside the handbag were these things: a lacy handkerchief; a ball of string; a bag of peppermints; some letters tied up with a ribbon; a big ball of wool; and a pair of knitting needles.

Billie loved Mrs Pinkerton-Trunks, and wherever Billie, Monkey and Mr Milford-Haven went, Mrs Pinkerton-Trunks went too. At night she sat on the windowsill in Billie's bedroom, and sometimes, just before she went to sleep, Billie thought she heard the click-click of the knitting needles, and the sound of Mrs Pinkerton-

Trunks's voice murmuring, 'Knit one, purl one and knit two more.'

'Is that you, Mrs Pinkerton-Trunks?' said Billie. But when she sat up in bed, she saw that Mrs Pinkerton-Trunks was sitting quite still on the windowsill, holding her handbag on her knee.

Then one day, when Billie was almost five, her father gave her a puppy dog. His name was Woodley, and he was small and white and heavy and warm. Billie lifted him from his basket, and he trotted over the kitchen floor and sniffed at the table legs. Then he turned and ran out into the garden. Billie put Monkey, Mr Milford-Haven and Mrs Pinkerton-Trunks into the little wooden wagon, and ran after him. Bumpitty-bump! went the wheels as she ran, tugging the wagon string behind her. Round and round the garden she went, following the white puppy, until at last he ran to the top of the hill and sat down beneath the three tall trees. Billie sat down beside him, and one by one the animals climbed from the wagon.

'I say!' said Mr Milford-Haven. 'That was a jolly fast ride!'

'I'm *quite* out of breath, dear!' said Mrs Pinkerton-Trunks.

Monkey said nothing at all – for the ride had given him hiccups. HIC!

Woodley's Holiday

Woodley always barked when the milkman came down the path, or when the postman brought the letters. 'Why do you do it?' asked Billie one Monday morning, when everyone was sitting having breakfast. 'Why do you always bark?'

'It's my job,' said Woodley. 'It's my job to let you all know when the milkman comes down the path, and when the letters arrive.'

Monkey stared at Woodley, and his eyes got bigger and rounder with excitement. '*I* want a job!' he said. '*I* want to tell everyone when the milkman comes down the path, and when the postman brings the letters.'

'You're much too young, dear,' said Mrs

12

Pinkerton-Trunks. 'That is a job for someone much older and wiser. Someone like myself.'

'I rather think that *I* would be quite good at the job,' said Mr Milford-Haven. '*I* should like to tell everyone when the milkman and the postman come down the path.'

They all jumped down from the table and hurried to the front door, pushing and jostling one another as they went. Woodley watched them go. 'I don't know what all the fuss is about,' he said. 'It's *my* job.'

Billie sat down beside him and put her arms round his neck. 'Couldn't you take a little holiday?' she whispered in his ear. And so it was decided that for the rest of the week Monkey, Mr Milford-Haven and Mrs Pinkerton-Trunks would do Woodley's job, while Woodley enjoyed a few days' rest.

The next day was Tuesday. Mr Milford-Haven sat on the doorstep and waited for someone to come down the path. As soon as he saw the milkman he hurried to the kitchen, where everyone was busy making breakfast.

'Excuse me,' he said politely, 'but I should like to inform you that the milkman has arrived.'

Woodley was sitting under the table and he poked his head out from beneath the cloth. 'That won't do,' he said. 'No one can hear you!'

13

Mr Milford-Haven cleared his throat. 'Excuse me,' he said, 'the milkman is coming down the path.'

But still no one heard him. They were all busy bringing the knives and forks from the drawer, and warming the teapot on the stove.

'THE MILKMAN'S HERE!' shouted Mr Milford-Haven. Everyone was so startled by the sudden noise that they dropped whatever it was they were carrying.

'There's no need to shout, dear,' said Mrs Pinkerton-Trunks.

Mr Milford-Haven went to sit under the table with Woodley. 'I don't think I care much for this job,' he said.

The next day was Wednesday. Mrs Pinkerton-Trunks settled herself by the door, and when she saw the milkman coming along the path, she hurried back to the kitchen. 'It's the milkman, dear,' she said. 'At least, I *think* it's the milkman. It *might* be the postman . . . .'

'Post!' called the postman, as Mrs Pinkerton-Trunks rummaged about in her handbag for her spectacles.

The next day was Thursday. It was a lovely day, and Mrs Pinkerton-Trunks, Monkey and Mr Milford-Haven went for a walk up the hill before breakfast. When they returned, Billie was picking up the letters from the mat, and Billie's father was collecting the milk bottles from the step. 'You all forgot to do your job!' said Billie.

The next day was Friday, and it was Monkey's turn to sit by the front door. As soon as he saw the milkman coming along the path he ran back into the kitchen. 'He's here! He's here!' he shouted. He became so excited that he gave himself hiccups. 'It's the – hic!' he said, as he sat down on the mat. 'The – hic . . . the hic-hic . . . !'

The next day was Saturday, and everyone was very glad when Woodley said that his holiday was over. They sat at the table and watched as he hurried from the kitchen. 'Postman's here!' they heard him bark. 'Milkman's here!'

Mr Milford-Haven smiled as he took a thick slice of buttered toast from the toast rack. 'I must say,' he said, 'Woodley does his job awfully well, doesn't he?'

The Window Cleaner

Billie and Woodley were busy one morning in Billie's bedroom. They were tidying her sock drawer – and they had just put all the socks in a big heap on the floor, when they heard the sound of Monkey's feet scampering up the stairs. 'There's a man with a ladder!' they heard him cry. 'A man with a ladder!'

Woodley dropped the sock which he was holding in his mouth, and looked at Billie. Then he marched to the bedroom door and looked out. 'It's the window cleaner,' he said.

But Monkey didn't hear him – he was running up and down the stairs, shouting, 'It's a thief! It's a burglar!'

16

His shouts brought Mrs Pinkerton-Trunks from the kitchen. She pushed open the letter box with her trunk and peeped out. Then she began to run round and round in circles. 'Help!' she cried. 'Help! There's a man with a ladder, coming down the path!'

'It's the window cleaner!' called Woodley, from the top of the stairs – but neither Monkey nor Mrs Pinkerton-Trunks paid any attention to him. Their shouts brought Mr Milford-Haven from the back garden.

'It's a man with a ladder,' cried Monkey. 'It's a lamb with a madder . . . !'

'It's a *what*?' asked Mr Milford-Haven. He pushed open the door and padded a little way along the path – then he turned, and ran back into the house again. 'There's a man with a ladder!' he said. 'He's climbing up to the windows. He must be a burglar!'

'It's the window cleaner!' shouted Woodley – but no one took any notice of him; they were all running about in circles, bumping into one another, and tripping over one another's tails.

Woodley began to make his way down the stairs. He had just reached the bottom, when suddenly Mr Milford-Haven cried, 'Follow me!', and everyone rushed up to the landing.

Woodley sighed – uhhh! – and climbed the stairs again.

17

When he reached the top, he found Monkey, Mrs Pinkerton-Trunks and Mr Milford-Haven in the bathroom. They were huddled together by the wash-basin, looking at the shadow of the window cleaner which moved across the pane of frosted glass.

'Dashed fellow's trying to get in!' said Mr Milford-Haven, and he leapt up on to the windowsill, and growled and swished his tail. The shadow vanished, and everyone breathed a sigh of relief.

Woodley grinned. 'I told you,' he said. 'It's the . . . !' But he got no further, for he found a big golden paw over his mouth.

'Listen!' said Mr Milford-Haven. In the silence which followed there came the sound of the ladder as it was propped against the wall.

'. . . id hu indow eaner . . . !' said Woodley, trying to breathe through Mr Milford-Haven's paw. 'Tap-tap' went the end of the ladder, as it came to rest against a window pane. Everyone rushed from the room, trampling over Woodley, and leaving him flat on the mat. 'It's the window cleaner,' he said – then he got up, shook himself, and went to see what was happening.

On the landing every bedroom door was open, and Monkey, Mrs Pinkerton-Trunks and Mr Milford-Haven were running from room to room.

'Clear off!' growled Mr Milford-Haven, as he ran.

'I'll give you such a wallop with my handbag!' cried Mrs Pinkerton-Trunks.

'Go away! Go away!' shouted Monkey.

Woodley watched as they raced to and fro – and then he took in a deep breath, and shouted as loudly as he could, 'QUIET!'

The animals stopped running and sat down in surprise.

'It's the man who comes to do the windows,' said Woodley. 'He makes them all clean and shiny.'

The animals looked at Woodley – then they looked at one another – then they trooped quietly down the stairs, murmuring to one another as they went.

'It's the man who cleans the windows, dear.'

'That's who *I* thought it was, actually . . . .'

'Me too – me too!'

Woodley went back into Billie's bedroom.

'What was all the noise about?' asked Billie.

'Nothing,' said Woodley. 'It was just the window cleaner.'

The Furry Caterpillar

Billie and the animals were sitting having breakfast one morning, when Monkey came running into the kitchen holding something in his hand. He stretched out his arm, and there on his palm was a big, green furry caterpillar. 'I've called him Walter,' said Monkey, 'and he's going to live with me for ever and ever!' He put the caterpillar down, and watched as it crept slowly over the cloth.

'But he can't live with you, Monkey dear,' said Mrs Pinkerton-Trunks. 'He must live on a leaf in the bush. That's his home – that's where all his family live.'

Monkey picked Walter up from the table, and

went out along the garden path. Billie and the animals watched as he put the caterpillar back into the bush. 'Goodbye, Walter,' they heard him say. Then he came back into the kitchen, sat down at the table, and stared at his boiled egg.

'You can visit Walter after breakfast,' said Mrs Pinkerton-Trunks. 'I'm sure he'll be very glad to see you.'

Monkey smiled, and began to eat his egg. Billie and the animals went out into the garden to pull up the weeds in the flowerbed. 'Hel-lo!' cried Mr Milford-Haven, as they passed the bush. 'I can see Walter!'

'I don't think you can, dear,' said Mrs Pinkerton-Trunks, 'because Walter is up here. I can see him quite clearly!'

'You're both wrong,' said Woodley. 'He's down here.'

Mrs Pinkerton-Trunks looked again at the caterpillar on the top of the bush. She bent and looked at Woodley's caterpillar – then she looked at Mr Milford-Haven's – and they were all exactly the same. Which one was Walter?

Billie held out a big leaf, and Mrs Pinkerton-Trunks carefully picked the caterpillars from the bush, so that they could be looked at more closely.

'One . . . two . . . three,' she said, as she laid them down. 'Four . . . five . . . six . . . !'

'Stop!' cried Mr Milford-Haven. 'There's no more room!'

Billie and the animals sat down on the grass, and looked at the leaf. It was full of caterpillars – and they all looked exactly the same. 'Right!' said Woodley, and he ran down the path and into the kitchen, where Monkey was eating his boiled egg. 'Monkey,' said Woodley, 'how green was your caterpillar?'

'As green as grass!' said Monkey happily.

Woodley went back to the bush, and looked at the caterpillars. They were all as green as grass.

Next, Billie ran down the path to the kitchen. 'Monkey,' she said, 'how big is your caterpillar?'

Monkey held up his hand and made a little space between his finger and thumb. 'This big,' he said.

Billie turned and ran back to the animals. 'Monkey's caterpillar is this big,' she said, holding up her finger and thumb.

So Mrs Pinkerton-Trunks began to measure the caterpillars with a little snippet of wool which she took from her handbag. But as soon as she touched the first caterpillar it curled up into a little ball. Mr Milford-Haven padded along the path into the kitchen, where Monkey was drinking his mug of milk.

'Is your caterpillar ticklish?' asked Mr Milford-Haven. 'That is, if one touched him with a bit of wool, would he do this?' He lay down on the rug and curled up into a big golden ball.

Monkey stared at him in amazement. 'I don't think so,' he said. 'Shall I try, and see?'

He began to rummage about in the kitchen drawer for a snippet of wool. Mr Milford-Haven jumped up and raced down the garden path. When he reached the bush he found Billie holding the leaf on which six caterpillars lay curled – hiding their faces.

'There's only one thing to do,' said Mrs Pinkerton-Trunks – and to everyone's surprise, she took the leaf and shook it gently over the top of the bush. 'One, two, three,' she said, counting the caterpillars as they dropped. 'Four, five . . . .'

Caterpillar number six was put on a leaf by itself, at the bottom of the bush; and when Monkey came scampering along the path, he saw Walter at once. 'Hello,' he said happily.

Rainy Day

On the morning of Woodley's birthday Billie
and Monkey woke very early. It was raining, and
the wind blew the raindrops against the window-
pane so hard that they made a rattling sound.

Billie got out of bed, pulled back the curtain,
and looked down on the garden. The path was
full of puddles, and the raindrops were so big
and fell so hard that each drop jumped up from
the ground again.

'Monkey,' said Billie, in a whisper, 'it's raining
cats and dogs.'

Monkey was sitting on the bed, sucking his
thumb – but when he heard Billie say 'cats and
dogs' he jumped up, and ran down the stairs

and out along the garden path. Billie ran after him, but she was too late to catch him. By the time she got to the door he was already on his way back to the kitchen. He was very wet indeed, and he stood on the kitchen tiles in a little pool of water. 'I didn't see any cats and dogs,' he said crossly. 'There weren't any cats and dogs.'

'Oh, Monkey,' said Billie, as she rubbed him with a towel. 'It's raining cats and dogs just means that it's raining hard.'

The sound of their voices woke Mrs Pinkerton-Trunks. 'It's raining, Mrs Pinkerton-Trunks,' said Billie. 'It's raining on Woodley's birthday. We shan't be able to have the birthday picnic.'

Mrs Pinkerton-Trunks took her umbrella and went outside to see if there was a patch of blue in the sky. But the sky was grey all over. Mrs Pinkerton-Trunks came back and put her umbrella in the sink, so that the rain wouldn't make another pool on the floor. 'It's pouring down, dear!' she said.

Billie and Monkey and Mrs Pinkerton-Trunks looked to where Woodley lay sleeping on the rug. He was smiling in his sleep. 'He's dreaming about the birthday picnic,' said Billie. 'He'll be so disappointed.'

'Perhaps it will have stopped raining by the time he wakes,' said Mrs Pinkerton-Trunks.

Billie and Mrs Pinkerton-Trunks began to

make the birthday picnic. They worked quietly so as not to wake Woodley. Monkey sat on the windowsill and waited for the sun to come out. But the sun stayed behind the clouds. By the time Mr Milford-Haven woke, the puddles on the path were much bigger, and all the flowers in the flowerbeds were beaten to the ground by the rain.

'Good heavens!' said Mr Milford-Haven. 'It's raining on Woodley's birthday! He'll be so disappointed not to have his birthday picnic!'

So Billie put on her wellingtons, her red mackintosh, and her big red rain-hat. Mrs Pinkerton-Trunks took her umbrella, and together she and Billie climbed to the top of the hill, to see if there was a dry patch under the trees. But every blade of grass was wet, and bright green, and shining. The raindrops fell from the leaves of the trees and on to Billie's hat – splot! Then they fell from the brim of her hat and on to her nose – plop! – and made her giggle. The raindrops fell on Mrs Pinkerton-Trunks's umbrella – pitter-pat. 'For myself, dear,' said Mrs Pinkerton-Trunks, 'I quite *like* the rain. It makes the plants grow.'

Billie and Mrs Pinkerton-Trunks climbed through the gap in the hedge to Mrs Pinkerton-Trunks's rose garden. They picked some roses for Woodley. The earth round the roses was dark and soft with rain, and Billie's wellingtons made deep footprints as she walked between the bushes. Holding the wet roses, Billie and Mrs Pinkerton-Trunks went back to the kitchen. Woodley opened an eye as they came in. 'It's my birthday,' he said, with a grin. 'It's my special day!'

He got up and went to the door, and Billie and the animals held their breath as he looked out. 'It's raining,' he said.

'It's pouring down!'

'It's raining cats and dogs!'

Then, to everyone's surprise, he ran off down the path. Billie and the animals stood at the door and watched him go. 'Yip! Yip! Yip!' they heard him shout, as he jumped in all the puddles.

'Weeeeee. . . !' he shouted, as he raced up and down the hill.

'Well,' said Mr Milford-Haven, 'some like a dry birthday, and some like a wet one. It's all a matter of what you *like*. What do you say, Mrs P?'

But Mrs Pinkerton-Trunks was no longer standing by the kitchen door. She was plodding down the garden path and jumping in all the puddles. SPLASH!

Marbles

One day, when the animals were rummaging about in the attic, Woodley found a dusty little bag of marbles. 'Here's an old bean-bag!' he said. He tossed it into the air, and it came down at Monkey's feet – THUD.

Monkey picked up the little bag and shook it. He shook it so hard that the string which was tied round it came undone, and the coloured glass marbles rolled over the floor. Some marbles ran into a corner, and others rolled along the wooden floorboards, in the little space between one floorboard and the next.

Mr Milford-Haven watched as the marbles came towards him. Chink-chink-chink, they went, as they came to a stop in a little row in front of him. 'I say!' he said. 'These are rather odd·beans. How does one cook them?'

'You boil them, dear!' cried Mrs Pinkerton-Trunks.

'I don't think they're beans,' said Woodley – but no one took any notice of him; they were busy gathering up the marbles, and hurrying down the attic stairs.

In the kitchen Mrs Pinkerton-Trunks put the marbles in a bowl of water. 'First you soak them, until they're soft,' she said, 'and then you cook them.'

Mr Milford-Haven sat at the table, holding his knife and fork. 'I *do* like beans on toast,' he said, '. . . and I really am very hungry. Ah – haven't they gone soft yet?'

He looked into the bowl, where the marbles lay in the water, all shiny, and each with a lovely swirl of colour in the middle. 'They really are very pretty beans,' he said.

Woodley was sitting under the table, thinking; and what he was thinking was this: those things in the pan are *not beans*. I don't know what they are, but they are not beans. He poked his head out from under the table, to see what was going on. Mr Milford-Haven was gazing into the bowl of water and prodding the marbles with his fork. They were very hard. 'Ahhh. . . !' he said. 'Yes!

. . . What we have here is not beans. It's sweets. Boiled sweets.'

Boiled sweets on toast? thought Woodley, under the table.

'Sweets!' cried Monkey, and before anyone could stop him, he snatched three marbles from the bowl, and ran out of the kitchen and up to the top of the hill.

When Monkey reached the top of the hill, he sat down and looked at the marbles. He turned them round and round in his fingers, and they weren't in the least bit sticky. He went back down the hill, to where Woodley sat by the kitchen door. 'Woodley,' said Monkey, 'they aren't sweets. They aren't sweets, and you mustn't eat them.'

'I wasn't going to,' said Woodley. 'I think they're balls – little bouncy balls.'

So Monkey dropped a marble on the ground – but it didn't bounce; it just rolled over the floor and came to rest by the table leg.

Mr Milford-Haven was still sitting at the table. He was chasing six marbles round and round his plate with his fork.

'Eat your beans, dear!' cried Mrs Pinkerton-Trunks.

'I can't,' said Mr Milford-Haven. 'They won't stay still.' He jabbed so hard at his plate that the marbles fell to the floor. They looked so pretty as they rolled over the kitchen tiles that Mrs Pinkerton-Trunks gave a little cry.

'Oh!' she said. 'They're beads! I shall thread them on a string, and wear them on Sundays!' But when she picked up the marbles, she couldn't find a hole to put the string through.

'Well,' said Woodley, 'they aren't beans, or sweets, or balls, or beads. I think they're absolutely useless.'

'No, they're not,' said Monkey. 'We could play a game with them. We could roll them over the floor, and make them bump into one another.'

'What a good idea,' said Mr Milford-Haven. 'We could call the game "Chink".'

'Or "Clink"!' said Mrs Pinkerton-Trunks.

'Oh, animals!' said Billie, who had come quietly into the kitchen. 'They're *marbles*! It's a game called marbles!'

Everything in its Place

Billie's father said that she must tidy her room. 'It's dreadfully untidy,' he said. 'I don't know how you ever find anything.'

Billie hated tidying her room. She went out along the garden path – stamp-stamp-stamp – and up the hill. Mrs Pinkerton-Trunks ran out after her. 'Come back at once, dear,' she called. 'Come and tidy your nice room.'

'Shan't!' shouted Billie, as she disappeared over the top of the hill.

Mrs Pinkerton-Trunks settled her shawl around her shoulders and went back into the house. Woodley, Monkey and Mr Milford-Haven watched as she plodded up the stairs. 'I don't know how the poor child ever finds *anything*,' they heard her say, as she went into Billie's bedroom.

'It must be awful not to be able to find things,' said Woodley.

'It must be so annoying not to know where anything *is*,' said Mr Milford-Haven.

One by one the animals crept up the stairs and peeped into Billie's room. It was very untidy. Books lay open on the carpet, and pieces of jigsaw lay scattered about the floor. Billie's clothes lay in a heap on the chair. The wastepaper basket had overflowed, and there were bits of paper everywhere.

Mrs Pinkerton-Trunks sat in the middle of the room. Her hat had slipped over one eye and she looked bewildered. 'I simply don't know where to begin,' she said.

Monkey put his arms round her neck and gave her a hug. 'We'll help you,' he said; and he and Woodley and Mr Milford-Haven started work at once. Monkey gathered up all the bits of paper and put them in the wastepaper basket. Then he climbed up the edge of the door and put the basket on top of the wardrobe.

Woodley began to tug at Billie's blue dungarees. He tugged and tugged until he had pulled them off the chair, then he dragged them under the bed, out of sight. When the dungarees were tucked away, Woodley went back for the dresses, the T-shirts, and the socks.

The room began to look much neater and tidier, which cheered Mrs Pinkerton-Trunks so much that she got up, straightened her hat, and began to collect the pieces of the jigsaw. But the side of the box was broken, and as soon as she put the pieces in they all fell out again. Mrs Pinkerton-Trunks looked round for a new place to put them. 'Just the thing, dear!' she said to Woodley. 'That will make such a nice little bag!' She took the pink sock which Woodley was carrying in his mouth, put the jigsaw pieces into it, and dropped it into a drawer.

While all this was going on, Mr Milford-Haven was busy gathering all the books together in a corner of the room. He put them one on top of another – picture books, puzzle books, alphabet books, drawing books. Monkey came down from the wardrobe to help.

It was fun making a great tower of books, and when the last book was in place, Monkey and Mr Milford-Haven sat down to admire their work.

'No time to stop!' cried Mrs Pinkerton-Trunks. 'We must have everything in its place before Billie comes back.' She began to pick up the pencils and crayons, and Monkey put them in two rows, along the bookshelves.

When Billie came into the room, she found the

animals sitting in a row on her bed, smiling at her. 'Oh, animals,' she said, 'you are kind – thank you!' She looked round her tidy room, and then she saw the great wobbling tower of books in the corner, and the legs of her dungarees, which were peeping from under the bed, and the rows of pencils and crayons on the bookshelves.

Billie waited until the animals had gone down for lunch, and then she quietly put everything back in its place – the books on the bookshelves, the pencils and crayons in the pencil box, and the clothes in the drawer.

But, even though she looked all round the room, she couldn't find the wastepaper basket. And it was an awfully long time before she found the pieces of her jigsaw in the toe of her pink sock.

Upside Down

One day Mr Milford-Haven thought that it would be nice if he made a special tea for Billie and the animals. He looked in the cookery book and read about making cheese on toast. But cheese on toast seemed very hard to make. I'll make a jelly! said Mr Milford-Haven to himself. He went to the cupboard, and began to rummage about. He soon found what he was looking for – a dish shaped like a rabbit.

Mr Milford-Haven was so pleased and excited that he ran into the garden to tell Billie and the animals all about the special tea. 'It's a jelly,' he said, 'shaped like a rabbit – a jolly sort of orange rabbit, lying on his back with his feet in the air.'

He turned, and padded back to the kitchen.

Woodley was lying in the bush, and he poked his head out and looked at Billie. 'A jolly rabbit with his feet in the air?' he said. Everyone hurried to the kitchen to see the rabbit for themselves.

They found Mr Milford-Haven pouring the jelly into the dish. 'There you are!' he said proudly.

Mrs Pinkerton-Trunks put on her spectacles to look. 'But his feet won't be in the air when you turn the dish over, dear,' she said. 'When the jelly has set, you turn the dish *upside down*.'

When everyone had gone back to the garden, Mr Milford-Haven sat down on the rug and waited for the jelly to set. The dish is the right way up, he thought, but the jelly rabbit inside the dish is *upside down*. He got up and climbed on to the table, to make sure. 'Yes – there he is,' said Mr Milford-Haven, 'lying in the dish, upside down, with his feet in the air.'

He walked round and round the dish, and looked at it. But the dish is the right way up, he told himself. It must be the right way up. If it was upside down, the jelly would fall out.

He jumped down from the table and went slowly along the garden path. 'Now let me see –' he muttered, as he went. 'Dish right way up – rabbit upside down. *Turn the dish over*. Dish upside down – rabbit upside down . . . . I don't think I've got that right . . . . Oh, bother,' he said. 'I wish I'd made cheese on toast after all.'

For the rest of the afternoon Mr Milford-Haven walked round and round the garden. Billie and the animals stopped their game as he padded along the path. 'Right way up,' they heard him mutter, as he went by. 'Upside down . . . .'

'Come and play!' said Billie, but Mr Milford-Haven merely murmured 'upside down' again, and disappeared amongst the trees at the top of the hill.

At the top of the hill Mr Milford-Haven sat down by the hollow trunk of the dead tree. After a little while Monkey scampered up the hill to sit by Mr Milford-Haven's side. 'Come and play!' he said.

'I'm busy thinking,' said Mr Milford-Haven, 'and what I am thinking about is this: an upside-down rabbit, in a right-way-up dish.'

'Oh . . . .' said Monkey.

Mr Milford-Haven turned and looked at him. 'It's the bit about *turning the dish over*,' he said, 'and making the rabbit the right way up. That's the bit that puzzles *me*.'

He got up and began to pace round the tree trunk. Round and round he went, and then he stopped and said, 'A-ha!'

'Monkey,' he said, as he began to scramble headfirst into the tree trunk, 'this tree is a jelly dish – and I'm a jelly, going into the dish – upside down!'

Monkey sat on the grass and looked at Mr Milford-Haven in astonishment.

'I'm a jelly rabbit in a dish!' came the voice of Mr Milford-Haven from the hollow tree, 'and I'm upside down!'

Then – 'Monkey,' he said, 'if the tree was upside down, I'd be the right way up ... wouldn't I?'

Monkey giggled. 'Yes,' he said.

Mr Milford-Haven scrambled from the tree trunk, covered in dead leaves and bits of moss. 'Thank goodness for that!' he said. Then together he and Monkey went down the hill to the kitchen, where Mrs Pinkerton-Trunks was turning the jelly dish upside down on a plate. Slowly she lifted the dish – and little by little, the jelly rabbit came into sight. He was sitting the right way up, with all four feet on the plate – and he tasted very good indeed.

Asking Questions

Mr Milford-Haven was sitting in the kitchen one sunny afternoon, when Billie and her father came in, carrying a big parcel. They sat down at the table, took off the wrapping paper, and opened the box. Inside were some little strips of wood. Mr Milford-Haven watched as Billie's father took them out and began to fix them together; and when he had finished, they looked like a little tree in winter – a tree without leaves.

'By Jove!' said Mr Milford-Haven. 'That's a nice little tree!'

'It isn't a *tree*,' said Billie. 'It's a mobile.'

'There you are!' Billie's father said. 'You can put the birds on all by yourself.' He went from the room, and Mr Milford-Haven got up and padded across the kitchen.

'Excuse me,' he said, 'I know what a mobile *is*, of course . . . but I seem to have forgotten *exactly* what it is . . . . What is it?'

But Billie was much too busy to answer questions. She was taking the little coloured birds from the box and hanging them from the strips of wood. Mr Milford-Haven sat down on the rug again. What is a mobile? he asked himself. And when it's all put together – what does it do?

As he sat and asked himself these mysterious questions, the kitchen door burst open, and in came Monkey, Mrs Pinkerton-Trunks and Woodley. They were playing at running straight through the house and out through the front door – but they paused for a moment to look at the mobile.

'How pretty, dear!' said Mrs Pinkerton-Trunks.

'It will look nice when it's up,' said Woodley.

Up? thought Mr Milford-Haven. Up where? Does it fly?

He looked at Billie – she was hanging a little yellow bird on a strip of wood. 'Billie,' he said, 'does it fly?'

'Hhhhmmm. . . .' said Billie.

Well, thought Mr Milford-Haven, as he tried

41

to settle himself on the rug, at least I know that it's called a mobile, and that it flies. But he couldn't fall asleep for trying to imagine what the mobile would look like when it was flying. It would look very strange. Mr Milford-Haven couldn't stop thinking about how strange it would look . . . and *how* did it fly? Did the birds carry it in their beaks, or did they hold it up with their wings? It was useless to try to sleep with all these questions buzzing about in his head.

He got up and went to the table. Billie was holding a little blue bird. It turned round and round on its hook. Billie blew on it, so that it spun faster and faster. 'Billie,' said Mr Milford-Haven, 'may I ask you a question?'

But Billie didn't hear him – she was gazing at the little blue bird and smiling. Mr Milford-Haven marched from the kitchen and up the hill, where Woodley, Monkey and Mrs Pinkerton-Trunks were sitting beneath the trees. They were all talking about the mobile.

'I think it's the prettiest I've ever seen!' said Mrs Pinkerton-Trunks.

'I wonder if Billie will put it up in her room,' said Woodley. 'What do you say, Mr Milford-Haven?'

'Oh, yes!' said Mr Milford-Haven. 'In her room – definitely. The only place for it, really. . . .' He was becoming rather flustered, and he felt a little foolish. Everyone in the world knows what a mobile is – except me – thought Mr Milford-Haven. 'Excuse me. . . .' he said, and he turned and raced down the hill.

'Billie,' he said, as he came panting into the kitchen, 'what is it? What is a mobile?'

Billie smiled, and pointed to where the mobile hung from the window frame. The window was open, and the breeze blew the birds round and round on the little strips of wood.

Mr Milford-Haven flopped down on the rug. 'So *that's* a mobile, is it?' he said. '*That's* what it does! It's very pretty . . . yes. . . .' And he curled himself up into a comfortable ball, and had his afternoon nap.

Gardening

Mrs Pinkerton-Trunks was very fond of gardening. There was nothing she liked better than to spend the day with her trowel, and her fork, and her little bit of carpet, which she used for kneeling on. 'Prodding and planting, and poking about amongst the bushes! That's what I like, dear!' she said to Billie.

Mrs Pinkerton-Trunks had her own garden – a rose garden, which stood on the other side of the hedge. Mrs Pinkerton-Trunks went there every day to look after her roses. Billie went with her because Mrs Pinkerton-Trunks needed a push to get her through the gap in the hedge.

One day, when Billie had pushed Mrs Pinkerton-Trunks through the gap in the hedge, she was surprised to see her making her way back, almost at once. 'There's so little to *do*, dear!' she said. 'The roses are all blooming, and there isn't a weed to be seen.'

'Why don't you pull up the weeds in the big flowerbed?' asked Billie.

Mrs Pinkerton-Trunks jumped up at once and plodded down the hill. Billie saw her spread out her piece of carpet and kneel down. 'Now Mrs Pinkerton-Trunks is happy again!' thought Billie, and she skipped over the hill to where Monkey, Woodley and Mr Milford-Haven were playing ball.

Mrs Pinkerton-Trunks sang as she worked. 'Tra-la, tra-lee!' she sang, as she pushed the end of her fork under the roots of the weeds and lifted them out of the ground. She worked hard – but, when she had moved right round the flowerbed, she saw the little wooden sign which stood in the earth. Mrs Pinkerton-Trunks took out her spectacles to read it. 'Mari-golds,' she read. 'Marigolds! Oh, dear – they weren't weeds – they were flowers. I've made a mistake.'

Mrs Pinkerton-Trunks sat down on the path and wondered what to do. She looked at the pile of plants. 'Everyone will see the marigold

45

plants,' she said. 'They'll know I've made a mistake. Silly old elephant, that's what they'll say. . . .'

She gathered up her fork and trowel, and her piece of carpet. She put the little plants in her handbag, and she hurried off down the path, to sit in the bush.

When she was hidden by the leaves, she took the plants out of her bag and looked at them. Their leaves were hanging straight down by their stems, and they didn't look at all as they had looked when they were standing in the flower-bed, waiting to grow.

Billie and the animals were running down the hill. Billie was surprised to see Mrs Pinkerton-Trunks's hat lying on the path. Woodley didn't see it at all; he stepped on it and made a dent in the top.

'I always think it's a mistake to leave a hat in the middle of the path,' said Mr Milford-Haven.

Billie looked round the garden for Mrs Pinkerton-Trunks – but she was nowhere to be seen. 'Mrs Pinkerton-Trunks!' she called – but there was no answer. She turned, and called Mrs Pinkerton-Trunks's name again and again, until Monkey got impatient and stamped his foot.

'*I* think it's a mistake to be late for tea!' he said.

46

Billie and the animals made their way along the path. As they passed the bush, they saw the tip of a grey tail sticking out from amongst the leaves. 'Mrs Pinkerton-Trunks,' said Billie, 'what are you doing?'

Mrs Pinkerton-Trunks came out of the bush and looked at Billie and the animals. 'I've made a silly mistake,' she said. 'I've pulled up all the marigold plants instead of the weeds. I'm a foolish old elephant. . . .'

Billie put her arms round Mrs Pinkerton-Trunks's neck and gave her a hug. 'No, you're *not*,' she said. 'We'll just put all the little plants back again!'

'It's not the end of the world,' said Woodley.

When the marigolds were standing in the flowerbed once more, Billie brought her watering can and gave them a drink. Soon they were standing up straight and nodding in the breeze. Mrs Pinkerton-Trunks put on her hat and plodded over the hill to water the roses in her garden. Billie went with her, to give her a push. *Dear* Mrs Pinkerton-Trunks! she said to herself, as the tip of the grey tail disappeared through the gap in the hedge.

Snap – Crackle – Pop!

There was a new cereal for breakfast. It stood on the table in its yellow box. Mrs Pinkerton-Trunks put on her spectacles to read the big, red letters.

'Snap – crackle – pop! That's the noise the cereal makes, dear,' she said.

Monkey became very excited. He jumped up and poured out some cereal. Rustle-rustle-rustle, it went, as it fell – and then, without a sound, it lay in a little pile in his bowl. Monkey was very disappointed.

'You have to put the milk on, dear,' said Mrs Pinkerton-Trunks, 'and then it goes snap – crackle – pop!'

Monkey jumped down from the table and ran to the front door, to fetch the milk. But the empty bottles still stood on the step. The milkman's late! thought Monkey. He ran to the gate and looked along the street – but it was quiet and empty. Monkey listened for the sounds of the milkman coming – the rattle of the bottles in the crate – but there was no sound at all. He went back to the kitchen and stared at his bowl of cereal.

Tick-tock, went the clock on the wall; it was almost eight o'clock. 'The milkman's not usually late,' said Mrs Pinkerton-Trunks.

Eight o'clock came, and still there was no sound of rattling milk bottles, nor the crunch of the milkman's boots on the path.

Monkey put some sugar on his cereal and put his spoon beside his bowl. He could hardly wait for the wonderful moment when Billie would pour the milk from the blue jug.

'My cereal will go snap – crackle – pop!' he said.

Mr Milford-Haven sighed. 'I'm glad I've got porridge,' he said. 'It just lies there quietly in the bowl. . . .'

Woodley poked his head out from beneath the table. 'I can't hear any snaps, crackles and pops,' he said.

'It won't go pop! until the milk's poured on,'

said Mrs Pinkerton-Trunks, 'and we haven't got any milk because the milkman's late, dear.'

So Woodley went down the path to see if he could see the milkman. He slipped through the gate and ran down the street. Empty milk bottles stood on every step. Woodley went back to the kitchen, where Mrs Pinkerton-Trunks was gazing into her cup of tea. 'I can't drink it without milk,' she said.

'I can't eat my porridge without milk,' said Mr Milford-Haven.

'I can't hear my cereal go snap – crackle – pop!' said Monkey.

Billie sat by Monkey's side, ate her boiled egg, and drank her fruit juice – if you are having egg and orange juice for breakfast, it doesn't matter how late the milkman is. Woodley lay under the table and crunched his biscuits – if you are a dog who eats biscuits for breakfast, it doesn't bother you at all if the milkman's late.

Mr Milford-Haven stared at his bowl. His porridge was growing cold and making a little hard crust on top. Mrs Pinkerton-Trunks gazed at her tea – it was getting cloudy, so that she couldn't see the tea-leaves at the bottom of the cup.

'If the milkman's any later,' said Mr Milford-Haven, 'we shan't get any breakfast at all!' And just as he spoke, everyone heard the click of the gate, the crunch of boots on the path, and the rattle of the milk bottles on the step.

Billie ran to the door and brought the milk to the kitchen. Mrs Pinkerton-Trunks poured herself a fresh cup of tea. Mr Milford-Haven stirred his porridge, so that the little crust was broken up. Billie lifted up the blue jug and poured the milk over Monkey's cereal. Snap! it went: snap – crackle – POP!

A Secret Party

Just before Billie's birthday the animals were planning a party for her – a secret party – Billie was to know nothing about it.

But it is very hard to make a party in secret; there would be sandwiches to be cut, and decorations to be hung. Mrs Pinkerton-Trunks decided that the best thing would be to get everything ready very early in the morning and hide it all in the cupboard under the stairs, until it was time for the party to begin. So Mrs Pinkerton-Trunks wound up her big alarm clock, and put it beside the wagon.

Early next morning the alarm went off – BBBRRRR! Mrs Pinkerton-Trunks, Monkey and

Mr Milford-Haven woke up and jumped out of the wagon. Woodley woke up on the rug and began to bark. Billie woke up in her bedroom and came downstairs into the kitchen. 'Today is my birthday!' she said.

The animals sat in a row on the rug and looked at her. 'Many happy returns of the day!' they said. 'Are you going back to bed now?'

'No!' said Billie. 'It's my birthday!' She opened the door and danced off down the garden path.

'There's only one thing to do,' said Woodley. 'Instead of hiding the party in the cupboard, we'll have to *make* the party in the cupboard.'

They hurried to the fridge and opened the door. There on the shelves stood a sponge cake, with jam in the middle, a box of ice-cream, a jelly on a dish, a pat of butter, and a jar of honey. The animals put all these things in the wagon. Mrs Pinkerton-Trunks took a loaf of bread from the bin, plates from the rack, and spoons and some decorations from the dresser drawer. Then everyone ran back across the kitchen floor for they could hear Billie coming along the path.

SLAM went the cupboard door, as Monkey closed it just in time. 'Monkey,' he heard Billie say, 'what are you doing!'

'Nothing,' said Monkey.

Well, it is difficult to make a party in secret; it

is even more difficult to make it in the dark; and it is almost impossible to make it *quietly*. Mrs Pinkerton-Trunks buttered the slices of bread without a sound – but the lid of the honey pot wouldn't come off. Mr Milford-Haven tried as hard as he could: 'MMMMMM-MUMFF!' he said, as he twisted the lid in his paws. 'OUFF! EEEEE-ROOW!'

'Animals,' said Billie, 'you *are* doing something. What is it?'

'Nothing,' said Mr Milford-Haven – then he opened the door a little way and held out the honey pot. 'I say!' he said. 'Could you open this, please?' Billie opened the pot and gave it back to him. 'Thanks awfully,' he said. SLAM – the cupboard door was closed again. But Billie could hear the excited whispers.

'My paws are all sticky!'

'Don't sit on the jelly!'

'Where's the cake? I can't find the cake!'

Billie giggled, and went to the gate, to wait for the postman to bring her birthday cards. When she came back, the cupboard door was open and the animals had gone. The floor of the cupboard was covered with breadcrumbs. There was a buttery knife propped up in a corner, and the empty honey pot lay on its side.

Billie went out into the garden and climbed to the top of the hill. There was no one there – but streamers and tinsel and coloured glass balls hung from the branches of the smallest tree. There was jelly and ice-cream, a cake and honey sandwiches set out on a cloth.

'Oh, animals!' said Billie.

One by one they came out from behind the trees, smiling shyly. 'It's your birthday party,' they said.

'We made it in secret.'

'Are you pleased?'

'Are you surprised?'

'Oh, I *am*,' said Billie. 'I'm very pleased – and I'm *very* surprised!'

Collecting Things

Woodley had always collected stones, of every shape and size. There were stones which looked like potatoes, and stones which looked like eggs. Some stones had many colours, but the colours could be seen only when the stones were wet. One by one, Woodley had found them, and had carried them to his kennel and put them in a corner. The piles of stones grew higher and higher until one day. . . .

'Billie,' said Monkey, 'Woodley's kennel is like this!' He stood on the kitchen rug and leant to one side.

'I think he means the kennel's falling down!' said Mr Milford-Haven.

Billie and the animals ran down the garden path. As they ran, they listened for the loud CRASH! of the falling kennel – but when they turned the bend in the path, they found the kennel still in one piece, but with three of its corners up in the air.

'Woodley!' shouted Billie.

'Yes?' said Woodley. He came to his doorway and looked out. And then he slowly slid from sight. Strange noises came from inside the kennel. CLUNK! BONK! RUMBLE! Mrs Pinkerton-Trunks snatched Monkey up, and held him in her trunk. Mr Milford-Haven took a step back-wards. Billie knelt in front of the kennel and looked inside. Woodley was sitting in the corner, on a great heap of stones. He looked like a big, furry bird, hatching some strange eggs. 'Oh . . . Woodley. . . !' said Billie.

'It's nothing to laugh about,' said Woodley. 'It's my collection. I keep my stones in a corner, but they are so heavy that my kennel's gone all skew-whiff.'

'Why don't you spread the stones out over the floor?' said Billie.

Woodley thought that this was a good idea. He began to trundle the stones over the kennel floor. Billie got up and went to where Mrs Pinkerton-Trunks and Mr Milford-Haven stood by the bush. 'Woodley's arranging his collection,' she said. Everyone breathed a sigh of relief, and went for a walk up the hill.

When they came down again, the kennel was now tilted over backwards. Woodley was looking out from his doorway. 'I put the stones in a row at the back of the kennel,' he said, 'and they tipped it up in the air. I can't get out.'

Mr Milford-Haven and Mrs Pinkerton-Trunks ran to the back of the kennel and began to push. Suddenly the kennel rolled over with a crash. **CLUNK! BONK! RUMBLE!** went the stones, as they rolled over the kennel floor. 'Ouch!' said Woodley, as he shot through the doorway.

It was plain to see that the collection couldn't be kept in the kennel any longer. 'I think the stones would look nice arranged on a shelf, dear,' said Mrs Pinkerton-Trunks.

And so the stones were loaded on to the wagon and taken to the house. Billie made a space on her shelf and began to set them out. Soon the shelf was full; but there were stones left over, waiting for a place where they could be seen and admired. 'Woodley,' said Billie, 'the collection is too big.'

'Just keep your favourite stones, dear!' said Mrs Pinkerton-Trunks.

Woodley sighed – uhhh! They were all his favourites: the stone with the little dimple, the stone with the pink streak, the stone which looked like a little cat.

One by one, the stones were collected together and taken back to the garden. Mrs Pinkerton-Trunks lifted the end of the wagon and tipped them out on to the ground. They looked so pretty, lying there, that she knelt down and began to arrange them in a pattern: first the smooth stones; then the stones which looked like potatoes; and the oddly shaped stones; and the stones which had many colours when they were wet.

When the last stone had been put in its place, Woodley walked round his collection. He was very pleased. 'Thank you!' he said to Mrs Pinkerton-Trunks – and then he turned and trotted up the garden path.

'Where are you going?' Billie called after him.

'To look for sticks,' said Woodley. 'You have made my collection of stones look so pretty that I want to make another one with sticks.'

A Day Out

Billie and the animals were going for a day out at the seaside. They travelled in a big red coach, with their lunch packed in a basket.

Billie and Mrs Pinkerton-Trunks, Woodley and Mr Milford-Haven had all been to the seaside before, and they knew exactly what it would be like. But Monkey had never, ever seen the sea, and he couldn't wait!

At last the coach stopped, and everyone got out. Billie and the animals began to walk to the sand dunes. Monkey ran ahead, over the soft, warm hills. 'I'm going to run into the sea!' he shouted, as he ran. 'I'm going to jump into the waves!'

But when he reached the top of the dunes, he stopped and stared. There was the sea, stretching out in front of him, and Monkey couldn't see the place where it ended.

'The sea!' cried Billie. 'The big, blue sea!' And down went the basket, the bucket and spade, the beach ball, and the towel!

Monkey watched as everyone ran over the golden sand, leaving rows of footprints behind them. *I'm* going to run into the sea, he said to himself, and get wet all over . . . but not just now.

He crouched down and began to make a little castle. He patted the sand down in the bucket, and then turned it over and made one of the towers. As he played he looked up from time to time, and saw Billie, Mrs Pinkerton-Trunks, Woodley and Mr Milford-Haven down by the edge of the sea. They were walking along in the sunshine and splashing through the waves. White birds flew over their heads, and the sea made a lovely sound, like a whisper. It is beautiful, thought Monkey, and he left his castle and began to walk over the sand.

I'm going to jump in the waves! he said to himself. I'm going to jump – SPLASH! – right into the sea! . . . but first, I'll collect some shells.

When Billie and the animals came back up the

beach, they found Monkey crouching by a little pool. There was a pile of shells by his side, and some strands of seaweed. Mrs Pinkerton-Trunks helped him carry them back to his castle. Then she took the towel and wiped the sand from his paws and feet. Billie spread out the cloth and got out the lunch.

As Monkey ate his lunch, he held a shell to his ear and listened to the sound of the sea – shooo-shooo. It was a friendly sound; but when Monkey looked at the sea, it made him shiver.

'Oh, I do like to be beside the seaside!' sang Mr Milford-Haven. 'I do like to stroll along the prom, prom, prom – where the brass band plays tiddly-om-pom-pom!'

But there was no cheerful brass band playing tiddly-om-pom-pom – only the quiet little beach and the big, blue sea that didn't seem to end anywhere.

After lunch Billie, Woodley and Mr Milford-Haven played with the beach ball. Monkey stayed close to Mrs Pinkerton-Trunks's side, and continued to build his castle. Tower upon tower he made – and as he patted the sand in his bucket, he listened to the sound of the sea. Higher and higher rose the castle, with turrets and walls. And one by one, first Billie, then Woodley, and then Mr Milford-Haven left their game and came to help. Billie decorated the walls with shells. Mr Milford-Haven stuck little flags on the tops of the towers; Woodley dug a moat and filled it full of water; and then the castle was finished. Billie, Woodley and Mr Milford-Haven lay down side by side. The sun was hot and made them sleepy.

'Tide's coming in. . . .' said Woodley.

'It's been a nice day out. . . .' said Mr Milford-Haven.

'Soon be time to go home. . . .' said Billie.

Monkey sat and gazed at the sea. The little waves were running up the beach and back again. Shooo-shooo, they said.

'Mrs Pinkerton-Trunks,' said Monkey, 'I'm going to paddle! I'm going to jump in the waves!' He got to his feet, and Mrs Pinkerton-Trunks put away her knitting. Then together, paw in trunk, they went down to the edge of the sea.

Flying

One sunny afternoon Mr Milford-Haven was lying on his branch on the tree in the garden. He was almost asleep, when a bee flew past his nose. BZZZZZZ! Mr Milford-Haven opened an eye and looked at the bee. He was a nice, fat, furry bee, and he bobbed up and down in the air, like a little ship at sea. Jolly little chap! thought Mr Milford-Haven, as he made himself more comfortable on the branch.

But he couldn't go to sleep for thinking about how nice it must be to fly through the air. He bounced up and down on his branch as he thought of it. 'To bob along on the breeze,' he murmured, 'up and down . . . and up and . . . WHOOOOPS!'

THUD! He landed at Mrs Pinkerton-Trunks's feet.

'Whatever are you doing, dear?' said Mrs Pinkerton-Trunks.

'I beg your pardon,' said Mr Milford-Haven, 'but I was thinking about flying.'

At this, Mrs Pinkerton-Trunks became very flustered. 'Oh!' she cried. 'Where were you thinking of flying to, dear? Have you got your ticket? You can't fly without a ticket, you know.'

A ticket? thought Mr Milford-Haven, as he went slowly down the hill. I thought I would need *wings* to fly. Birds have wings – bees have wings – everything that flies has wings.

For the rest of the afternoon he walked round and round the garden, trying to find a creature without wings – and who flew with a ticket. Down by the pond he saw a dragonfly, skimming over the water. But the dragonfly didn't seem to have a ticket – just a pair of big gauzy wings.

Mr Milford-Haven sat down on the grass. It must be wonderful, he thought, to skim over the water in the sunshine. He wondered, if he flapped his two front paws, would he be able to fly like the dragonfly or the bee? But no matter how hard he flapped, his two back paws stayed firmly on the ground. Mr Milford-Haven was disappointed and out of breath. Mrs P is right, he thought, I need a ticket – wings *and* a ticket. He got up and padded down the hill to the kitchen, where the coats hung on their hooks by the door. Mr Milford-Haven felt in all the pockets until he found what he wanted – a ticket!

Mr Milford-Haven took his old bus ticket up to the top of the hill. On the path at the bottom of the hill he could see Billie and the animals walking home for tea. But *I* shall fly! thought Mr Milford-Haven. I shall float down the hill! How surprised they'll all be!

'One!' he cried, holding his ticket tightly. 'Two!' he said, raising his paws in the air. 'Three!'

And nothing happened – nothing at all. 'THREE!' he shouted again – but no matter how he flapped, or waved his ticket in the air, his two back paws stayed firmly on the ground. He walked down the hill, and home for tea. He sat at the table, but felt too sad to eat his buttered scone, and left it uneaten on his plate.

In the evening Billie took him for a walk round the garden, to cheer him up. 'Billie,' he said, as they wandered up the hill, 'can *people* fly?'

'Only in an aeroplane,' said Billie. 'First you buy your ticket – then you get on the plane – and then you fly.'

'Ah. . . .' said Mr Milford-Haven. 'Bit like a bus, I suppose. . . .'

He lay down in the long grass, and a cloud of tiny insects came and danced round his head. They were very small, and there were so many of them buzzing round that it seemed as if he was wearing a veil. He got up and together he and Billie walked back down the hill. There they are, he said to himself, flitting up and down on their little wings . . . .

It was a pity that lions didn't have wings. It was a pity that they couldn't buzz and flit through the air.

'My paws are firmly on the ground,' he said. 'But, on the other hand . . . I could always buy myself an aeroplane ticket!'

And with that, he went back into the house, and ate his buttered scone.

Mrs Pinkerton-Trunks Sings

One day Mrs Pinkerton-Trunks said that the thing she wanted to do most was to give a song recital on top of the hill. Everyone agreed that it would be lovely to sit on top of the hill in the sunshine and listen to some singing. Mrs Pinkerton-Trunks was pleased – and a little flustered. She pinned a rose to her shawl, and took out her best lace handkerchief, waving it gaily in her trunk as she plodded up the hill. Billie and the animals climbed up behind her, sat down on the grass, and waited for the songs to begin.

Mrs Pinkerton-Trunks said she must first

practise some scales. 'Doh!' she sang. 'Doh ray me fa so la te doh! Doh te la so fa me ray doh!' It was lovely how her voice climbed higher and higher, right up to doh, and then back down again.

'That was a jolly nice song,' said Mr Milford-Haven. 'It was just like climbing up the hill, and then going down the other side.'

'Oh, that wasn't a *song*, dear,' said Mrs Pinkerton-Trunks. 'I haven't yet decided which song to sing.'

'Sing a lullaby,' said Monkey – and so Mrs Pinkerton-Trunks sang 'Rock-a-by-baby, in a tree top. . .'. Her voice was soft and low, like a summer breeze blowing through the trees.

'Aaaa-uuummmm. . . .' said Mr Milford-Haven, and he closed his eyes. Monkey cuddled up to Billie's side, and soon everyone was asleep in the grass.

'Ahem!' said Mrs Pinkerton-Trunks.

'AHEM!' she said again, and everyone opened their eyes.

'That was delightful,' said Mr Milford-Haven, 'but I think you should sing a *rousing* sort of song.'

So Mrs Pinkerton-Trunks sang 'The Grand Old Duke of York'. Mr Milford-Haven beat time with his paw on his knee. 'Oh, the *grand* old duke of *York* – he *had* ten thousand *men*. . . !' Then he

69

got to his feet and began to march down the hill. Soon Billie, Monkey and Woodley were marching behind him. Down to the path they went – tramp-tramp-tramp. 'Come back!' cried Mrs Pinkerton-Trunks.

When everyone was sitting on top of the hill again, Woodley said, 'I think you should sing a lively song. A lively song – but not a marching song.'

Mrs Pinkerton-Trunks thought for a moment, and then she began to sing. 'Tar-ra-ra-BOOM-de-ay!' she sang. 'Tar-ra-ra-BOOM-de-ay. Tar-ra-ra-BOOM-de-ay!   Tar-ra-ra-BOOM-de-ay!' Soon they were all up on their feet again and dancing wildly through the long grass. 'Tar-ra-ra-BOOM-de-ay!' they shouted as loudly as they could, and they danced until they were out of breath, and Monkey had hiccups. Woodley lay panting by the bench, with his tongue hanging out. 'That *was* a lively song,' he said. 'I think you should sing something quiet and slow now.'

Everyone agreed that this was the best thing to do, and they climbed back to the top of the hill and sat down in a row. Mrs Pinkerton-Trunks began to sing, 'All the birds of the air fell a-sighing and a-sobbing, when they heard of the death of poor cock-robin. . . .'

'Sniff. . . !' said Monkey, wiping a tear from his cheek. Mrs Pinkerton-Trunks gave him her lace handkerchief to dry his eyes.

'Perhaps I shouldn't sing that song, dear,' she said. 'It's a little bit sad.'

Mrs Pinkerton-Trunks sat down under the trees and wondered which song she should sing next. She had sung a lullaby, a song which was good for marching to, and a very lively song. She had sung a sad song. There was just one more song she knew, and it was the song she liked the best. 'I'm called little Buttercup,' she sang softly beneath the trees, 'dear little Buttercup, though I shall never know why. But still I'm called Buttercup, dear little Buttercup, sweet little Buttercup, I!'

Everyone liked this song so much that they sang it all the way home for tea.

'Sweet little Buttercup,' sang Billie and Woodley.

'Dear little Buttercup,' sang Mr Milford-Haven.

'Sweet little Buttercup, I!' sang Monkey.

The Bicycle

There was a big, flat parcel propped up in the hall of Billie's house. It had Billie's name on it – it was wrapped in brown paper – and no one knew what was inside.

Billie had gone for a long walk with Woodley and Monkey. Mr Milford-Haven and Mrs Pinkerton-Trunks sat and stared at the parcel. The paper was torn at one corner, and Mr Milford-Haven bent and peeped inside. 'It's a hoop!' he said.

'Nonsense, dear!' said Mrs Pinkerton-Trunks. 'It's much too big to be a hoop!' She felt inside the parcel with the tip of her trunk. 'It's a wheel,' she said.

'Rubbish!' said Mr Milford-Haven. 'It's a hoop, I say!'

Mrs Pinkerton-Trunks carefully prodded her trunk down inside the parcel once more. 'It *is* a wheel,' she said. 'I can feel the spokes.' Then – 'Goodness gracious!' she exclaimed. 'I can feel another wheel – a little wheel. It's a penny-farthing bicycle!'

Mrs Pinkerton-Trunks and Mr Milford-Haven climbed to the top of the hill to wait for Billie to come home. As they went, Mrs Pinkerton-Trunks thought about her great-grandfather. He had ridden a penny-farthing bicycle when he was young. He rode along in the sunshine, she thought to herself. How wonderful it must have been . . . how dignified he must have looked! Except when he fell off, of course!

The idea of her great-grandfather falling off his bicycle made Mrs Pinkerton-Trunks giggle, and she told the story to Mr Milford-Haven.

Mr Milford-Haven listened carefully to the story of how Mrs Pinkerton-Trunks's great-grandfather fell off his bicycle. She told him all about the big wheel at the front, and the little wheel at the back, and of how the spokes sparkled in the sunshine as the wheels went round and round.

It sounded a lot more fun than a hoop, thought Mr Milford-Haven; except for the bit about falling off. 'By Jove!' he said. 'I hope it *is* a penny-farthing bicycle in Billie's parcel!' And he padded down the hill and into the house to have another look. He prodded the torn corner, and then he pushed his paw inside. RIII-IIP! went the brown paper.

Mr Milford-Haven stared at the half-opened parcel, and then he turned and ran back up the hill, as fast as he could. 'Mrs Pinkerton-Trunks,' he said, 'it isn't a penny-farthing bicycle. It's a *squashed* bicycle.' He put his two front paws together to show Mrs Pinkerton-Trunks how the wheels lay together in the parcel. 'Two big wheels, and two little wheels, all squashed together – like this!'

Mrs Pinkerton-Trunks jumped to her feet and hurried down the hill. 'Oh, the poor child!' she said, as she ran. 'How disappointed she'll be! We must unsquash it as quickly as we can!'

When Mrs Pinkerton-Trunks reached the bicycle, she poked her knitting needle between the wheels – but try as she might, they wouldn't come apart. Mrs Pinkerton-Trunks sighed and sat down on the bottom stair. Mr Milford-Haven sat by her side and tried to think of a way to un-

74

squash a bicycle. He thought for a whole five minutes, but still he couldn't think how it might be done.

CLICK went the catch on the garden gate, and Billie came skipping along the path. Mrs Pinkerton-Trunks jumped to her feet and went to the door to meet her. 'I'm afraid your new bike is squashed, dear,' she said – but she spoke so gently that Billie didn't hear. RIII-IIP! went the brown paper, as Billie finished unwrapping the parcel.

'Try not to be *too* upset,' murmured Mrs Pinkerton-Trunks. 'Mr Milford-Haven is thinking of a way to unsquash it. . . .'

But Billie didn't seem at all upset. She was looking at her new bike and smiling. She touched the shiny handlebars and the spokes of the wheels. She rang the bell – BBBRRRR-INK! And then she took hold of the bike – and unfolded it! The two big wheels came apart, like the pages of a book, and the two small wheels came out from the side of the bike on two little brackets.

Billie wheeled her bike out along the garden path, and Mr Milford-Haven smiled as he saw the silvery spokes shining in the sun. 'There you are!' he said to Mrs Pinkerton-Trunks. 'No problem!'

But Mrs Pinkerton-Trunks was no longer

75

sitting on the stair. She was hurrying along the path, behind Billie. 'Be careful, dear!' she called, as she ran. 'Be careful not to fall off! Remember my great-grandfather . . . !'

Where is Tortoise?

It was winter. Most of the leaves had fallen from the trees. The bracken on the hill had turned brown. It was so cold that Billie and the animals could see their own breath, floating out from their mouths like little clouds. The sky was grey and full of snow – but everyone was much too busy to think about making a snowman. They were looking for the tortoise.

His disappearance was very strange. He had lived in the garden for just a few days, and he had seemed happy. He didn't say a lot – well, nothing at all, in fact – but whenever he poked his head out from his shell, he looked as if he

77

was smiling. And then – quite suddenly – he was gone.

Mrs Pinkerton-Trunks thought that perhaps he had gone to visit his relatives. But three whole days went by and he didn't return.

'What we must do,' said Woodley, 'is get up a search party. We must go to the top of the hill and call his name, very loudly.'

But this was impossible. The tortoise hadn't been given a name; for no one could agree what the name should be.

'How sad,' said Mrs Pinkerton-Trunks, as she climbed the hill. 'How very sad, to be lost in the wintertime, without a name.'

'And without a woolly hat and mittens,' said Monkey.

'And no little house to sleep in,' said Billie.

They called, as loudly as they could, 'Tortoise! Tortoise!' But there was no answer. 'Tortoise, where are you?' But still there was no answer. So everyone went down to the garden shed to get warm.

Inside the shed the windows were covered with frost. It made patterns like leaves and ferns and trees. Billie and Woodley breathed on the glass and the frost was melted by their warm breath. Woodley rubbed a little clear space with his paw, so that he could look out into the garden.

Mrs Pinkerton-Trunks sat down on a seed box and thought about the spring, and the warm sunshine, and of how she would dig little holes in the earth, with her trowel, to plant the new seedlings.

Mr Milford-Haven said, 'I think it's strange that some birds fly away as soon as it's winter-time.'

'Perhaps tortoises go away in the wintertime as well,' said Monkey.

But Mrs Pinkerton-Trunks just said, 'Don't be silly, dear!' and pulled his woolly hat down over his head, to keep his ears from freezing.

'I think it's strange how the earth goes hard in winter,' said Woodley. 'You can't find a soft spot to bury anything!' He picked up a bone from the corner of the shed and ran out along the path.

Billie looked through the window and saw him race to the top of the hill. She watched as he scrabbled in the leaves – and then he stopped, and lay on his tummy and wagged his tail. 'Billie!' he barked. 'Mrs Pinkerton-Trunks!'

Billie and the animals ran to the top of the hill – and there was the tortoise, lying among the leaves which Woodley had turned over. He looked comfortable and drowsy. 'He says he's going to sleep for the winter,' said Woodley. 'He says he does it every year. It's called hibernating.'

Everyone was very pleased that the tortoise

was safe and well, and Mrs Pinkerton-Trunks began to sprinkle dried leaves back over his shell. When the last leaf was patted gently into place, everyone began to make their way home for tea. Halfway down the hill Monkey turned and waved his paw. 'Goodbye!' he called. 'Good-by, Wilbur!'

'No, no, dear!' said Mrs Pinkerton-Trunks. 'His name isn't Wilbur – it's Arthur.'

'No, it isn't,' said Billie. 'It's Fred.'

'It's George,' said Mr Milford-Haven firmly.

'Well, you're all wrong,' said Woodley, with a grin. 'It's Rover!'

Hide and Seek

Billie and the animals were playing hide and seek. It was Woodley's turn to try and find them. He closed his eyes and counted to ten, very slowly. While he counted, Monkey ran round the other side of the hill; Mr Milford-Haven scrambled up the trunk of his tree; while Mrs Pinkerton-Trunks and Billie went to hide under a great clump of bracken. Sitting there was just like being in a little green tent.

'I *do* like a nice game of hide and seek, dear,' said Mrs Pinkerton-Trunks. 'It's so peaceful and I can have a little snooze!'

She made her shawl into a pillow, and pulled her red hat down over her eyes. But, before she could go to sleep, she heard a strange little noise. Billie heard it too. Pitter-patter, pitter-patter. Then it stopped. It came again. Pitter-patter, pitter-patter. Then they heard a sad little voice. 'I can't find a place,' it said. 'Where's a little place . . . ?'

Billie and Mrs Pinkerton-Trunks lifted a frond of bracken and peeped out. There, running through the long grass, was Monkey. Mrs Pinkerton-Trunks stretched out her trunk and pulled him in with them. 'Oooo!' said Monkey, who was very surprised.

'Hush!' said Billie. 'Woodley will hear you!'

When Monkey was sitting quietly, everyone made themselves comfortable and listened to the sound of the birds in Mr Milford-Haven's tree. The birds called to one another and sang little tunes. One sang 'A little bit of bread and no cheese', over and over again. Well, that's what it sounded like.

Billie looked out from the bracken, but all she saw was the tip of Mr Milford-Haven's tail hanging down from the branch. 'Mr Milford-Haven,' she whispered, 'pull up your tail! Woodley will see it!'

'Thanks awfully!' came the voice of Mr Milford-Haven from the tree.

When Mr Milford-Haven's tail was tucked away out of sight, everyone waited patiently for

Woodley to find them. They could hear him barking, but the sound seemed to come from far away. 'I say!' called Mr Milford-Haven. 'I can see Woodley! He's running down the lane and into the wood.'

Billie, Monkey and Mrs Pinkerton-Trunks came out of the bracken and began to make their way down the hill. Mr Milford-Haven jumped from his tree and followed them, and everyone shouted as loudly as they could.

'Woooooodley!'

'We're in the garden!'

'Come back, old chap!'

'Yoo-hoo, dear!'

But Woodley was too far away to hear. Billie and the animals sat down on the bench. They had not been waiting long when they heard the click of the gate, then the sound of paws on gravel, and then Woodley came into view. He grinned and wagged his tail when he saw Billie and the animals.

'I don't think the bench is a good hiding place,' he said. 'I can see you all quite clearly. And now that I've found you, it's *my* turn to hide!'

Before anyone could stop him, he turned and raced up the hill. Yip! Yip! Yip! he barked noisily as he went. Billie and the animals listened to his happy sound.

But as Woodley disappeared over the top of the hill the sound became fainter – Yip! Yip! Yip! – and fainter – Yip!

Until it couldn't be heard at all.

Making Parcels

It was Billie's father's birthday – and what he wanted most of all was a besom broom, to sweep the leaves from his lawn. 'Then we shall make him one, dear!' said Mrs Pinkerton-Trunks.

A besom broom is a broom that has twigs instead of bristles. Billie and the animals went into the wood to collect the twigs. When they had collected enough, Mrs Pinkerton-Trunks found a strong straight branch, and tied the twigs to the end with a long piece of string.

When the broom was made, Billie took hold of one end and Monkey took hold of the other. Then together they carried the broom to the house and hid it in the cupboard under the stairs.

'Aren't you going to wrap it?' asked Woodley. 'All birthday presents are wrapped in paper, with "Happy Birthday" and "Best Wishes" on them.'

'And a ribbon bow, dear!' said Mrs Pinkerton-Trunks. 'The parcel must have a nice ribbon bow.'

Billie and the animals began to look for a piece of paper to wrap round the broom. They found an old piece of Christmas wrapping paper – but that had 'Merry Christmas!' written on it.

'Perhaps we could cross out "Christmas" and write "Birthday" instead,' said Mr Milford-Haven. But 'Merry Birthday!' didn't sound quite right – and besides, no one knew how to write 'Birthday'.

Mrs Pinkerton-Trunks hurried upstairs, and came back with a length of red ribbon and a big sheet of tissue paper, which she kept wrapped round her best shawl. It was lovely paper. It was so thin that Billie could see her hand through it – and it made a wonderful rustling sound when she spread it out on the cupboard floor. But as soon as the broom was wrapped, the sharp ends of the twigs came through the paper.

'It does look a little strange,' said Mr Milford-Haven.

'You can see what's inside!' said Monkey. 'It won't be a surprise.'

'What we need is brown paper,' said Mr Milford-Haven. 'That's the thing for parcels – brown paper and string.'

So Billie went to the kitchen drawer and got a sheet of brown paper. But no matter how hard everyone tried, the paper wasn't big enough to cover the broom. They wrapped the brown paper round the branch, and the twigs stuck out of the top of the parcel. They wrapped the paper round the twigs, and the branch stuck out of the bottom of the parcel. Everyone sighed – uhhh! – and sat down on the floor of the cupboard.

'Newspaper!' said Woodley. 'Old newspapers – that's all we've got left to try!' He sounded quite disgusted – but it was a wonderful idea! Mrs Pinkerton-Trunks spread out the sheets and began to wrap them carefully round the broom. First the twigs were covered, and then the branch. Billie stuck the edges of the newspaper together with sticky tape, and Monkey tied on the big red bow.

When the parcel was made, Billie propped it in a corner of the cupboard, and everyone sat down and gazed at it.

'It's a delightful parcel, dear!' said Mrs Pinkerton-Trunks.

'You can't see what's inside it!' said Monkey.

'It's covered in words!' said Woodley. 'Hundreds of words!'

'And I'm sure that some of them must say "Happy" and some of them must say "Birthday"!' said Mr Milford-Haven.

In the News

Every morning the newspaper boy brought a newspaper to Billie's house. He pushed it through the letterbox, and it lay on the mat until Woodley carried it into the kitchen and gave it to Billie's father.

Billie's father was always very pleased to get his newspaper. 'Thank you, Woodley!' he said – and then he opened his paper, shook it, folded it, propped it against the milk jug, and read it. And no matter what Billie said to him after that, he just said, 'Hhhhmmm. . . .'

'Daddy, my bicycle tyre's gone flat!'

'Hhhhmmm. . . .'

'Daddy, the buckle's come off my sandal!'

'Hhhhmmm. . . .'

It made Billie very cross indeed. One morning she became so cross that she went away and sat on the garden bench. Mrs Pinkerton-Trunks, Woodley, Monkey and Mr Milford-Haven came to sit by her side.

'Don't be cross with your father, dear,' said Mrs Pinkerton-Trunks. 'Newspapers are very interesting to read.'

'They've got lots of pictures!' said Monkey.

'They tell you what's happening everywhere in the world!' said Mr Milford-Haven.

'Don't care!' said Billie. She jumped down from the bench and went to sit at the top of the hill. After a little while, she saw her father come out from the kitchen and sit down beside the garden shed. He was carrying his newspaper, and he opened it, shook it, folded it, and began to read it.

'Silly old newspaper!' shouted Billie – but no one heard her. Her father was hidden behind his paper, and the animals were walking along the path, talking to each other. Billie went into her playhouse and slammed the door shut – BANG!

Billie stayed in the playhouse for the rest of the morning. She drew some pictures and then she painted some patterns in her painting book.

It was almost time for lunch, when she heard the sound of the animals running up the hill.

'Extra! Extra!' they shouted. 'Read all about it!'

Billie opened her door and looked out. 'Read all about *what?*' she said.

'All about what's happened in the garden!' said Monkey. He dropped a big white sheet of paper at Billie's feet. Billie bent and picked it up. It was folded in half, to make two pages, and both pages were covered with pictures.

'It's got all the latest news, dear!' said Mrs Pinkerton-Trunks.

Billie sat down and looked at the newspaper. On the front page was a picture of Mrs Pinkerton-Trunks in her rose garden. She was pointing to a bush, where ten big red roses had opened their petals. 'Mrs Pinkerton-Trunks!' said Billie. 'Your roses have bloomed!'

On the next page was a picture of Woodley sitting by a hole in the garden. He was holding a bone in his mouth. 'Woodley!' said Billie. 'You found your bone!'

The next picture was of Monkey and Mr Milford-Haven, sitting on a branch of a tree. ' "Monkey and lion climb the highest tree in the world!" ' read Monkey. 'That's what the story says!'

On the last page was a picture of Billie's

father. He was sitting by the shed. His newspaper was on his knee – and there was a strange lump on his nose.

'This story says, "Billie's father stung by bee",' said Mrs Pinkerton-Trunks.

Billie got up and ran down the hill and into the kitchen. 'Daddy!' she said, as she gave him a hug. 'Poor daddy – stung by a bee!'

'How did you know?' asked her father.

'It was in my newspaper!' said Billie.

A Lost Puppy

One morning Billie and the animals found a small, spotted puppy in the garden. He was running through the long grass on the top of the hill – and all he would say was, 'Lost! Lost! Lost!'

Monkey went to him and tried to pat him. But the puppy ran away, backwards. 'Lost!' he said. 'Lost! Lost!'

Because he was running backwards, he couldn't see where he was going, and he ran into Mr Milford-Haven.

'There, there,' said Mr Milford-Haven. 'What's your name, little chap?'

'Lost!' said the puppy.

'Dashed odd name,' said Mr Milford-Haven. 'Are you sure it isn't Charlie – hhhmmm? Or Bertie, perhaps?' But the puppy just stared and began to walk backwards again. Mrs Pinkerton-Trunks scooped him up in her trunk and began to cuddle him.

'LOST!' yelped the puppy in her ear.

Mrs Pinkerton-Trunks was so startled that she dropped him. FLUMP! The puppy landed at Monkey's feet. Monkey smiled.

'Come and play!' he said, but the puppy just turned tail and ran down the hill.

He was so small that very soon he was hidden by the long blades of grass. Billie and the animals ran after him, but all they could see was sometimes the tip of his white tail, and sometimes the tips of his white ears when he jumped up into the air. It was impossible to catch him. Billie and the animals sat down on the top of the hill and watched as the puppy ran up and down. 'Lost! Lost! Lost!' they heard him shout.

'Poor little dear!' said Mrs Pinkerton-Trunks. 'What he wants is a comforting cuddle!'

'What he wants is a friendly pat,' said Monkey.

'What he wants is a name,' said Mr Milford-Haven.

'What he wants is a policeman,' said Woodley.

'Well – really, dear!' said Mrs Pinkerton-

Trunks. But Woodley just grinned and marched down the hill, through the gate and out along the street.

The garden grew very quiet and still after Woodley had gone. There were no little cries to be heard, and no one could see the white tips of ears or tail. 'I say!' said Mr Milford-Haven. 'I think the little chap's got lost again!'

Billie and the animals got up and began to look for the puppy. They found him fast asleep at the bottom of the hill. He was curled up into a little spotted ball, and he slept so soundly that he didn't hear the tramp-tramp-tramp of boots as the policeman came up the path with Woodley.

When the policeman saw the puppy, he smiled and gave him a friendly pat. Then he read the name tag on the puppy's collar. 'He's called Pip,' said the policeman, 'and he lives down the road.'

Billie and the animals went to the gate and watched as the puppy was carried back to his owner.

'Oh, he's so sweet!' cried Mrs Pinkerton-Trunks.

'He's so cuddly!' said Monkey.

'He's so small!' said Billie.

'So spotted!' said Mr Milford-Haven.

'And much too young to be out on his own!' said Woodley.